SAMMY THE GNAT

Gets a New Raincoat

Fly high!
Mo Silas

WRITTEN BY MORGAN SILAS DONNELLY
ILLUSTRATED BY KINSEY POULSON

Copyright © 2024 by Morgan Donnelly.

All rights reserved. No part of this book may be reproduced or used in any manner without written permission of the copyright owner except for the use of quotations in a book review. For more information, contact: sammy@SammyTheGnat.com

ISBN HARDCOVER: # 978-1-7382574-2-3
ISBN PAPERBACK: # 978-1-7382574-1-6
ISBN ELECTRONIC: # 978-1-7382574-0-9

Illustrator: Kinsey Poulson
Publishing Consultant: PRESStinely - PRESStinely.com

Portions of this book are works of fiction. Any references to historical events, real people, or real places are used fictitiously. Other names, characters, places and events are products of the author's imagination, and any resemblance to actual events or places or persons, living or dead, is entirely coincidental.

Printed in the United States of America.

MORGAN SILAS DONNELLY
sammy@SammyTheGnat.com
SammyTheGnat.com

DEDICATION

In honor of my mother, for singing lullabies to help me sleep.
Yeah, I remember.

In honor of my father, for telling me "Everything has a place,
and everything in its place."

To Molly, for giving me unconditional love. I hope you are getting
plenty of kibbies up there in dog heaven.

Lastly, to my muse, who helped the words flow
easily onto the pages.

Meet Sammy.

Sammy is a teeny-tiny gnat. He spends many hours happily flying with his family and friends in a gnat cloud under the warm summer sun.

Sammy loves flying in the wide-open spaces of the park where his family lives. There are tall trees and lots of green grass to play hide and seek in!

One Saturday, Sammy was playing baseball with his friends and teammates in the park. They had a big game coming up and they all wanted to practice for it.

Sammy saw his mom as she was coming home from shopping. She was carrying an extra big bag and it had something bright yellow in it. Sammy waved and she smiled back. Soon it was dinner time. After saying goodbye to his friends, Sammy went home.

After dinner, Sammy's mom asked him if he wanted a surprise, and he said, "Yes please!"

She pulled out a very unusual looking coat! It was slick and bright yellow! Sammy had never seen one like it. It was called a "raincoat," whatever that means!!!

Sammy had never seen rain before; only warm sunshine.

"The weather forecast for your first week of school is rain everyday. You can not fly if you are cold and wet, so the raincoat will keep you warm and dry," said Sammy's father.

Sammy can't fly when he is cold and soggy!

Sammy told his mother he did not like the coat! It smelled funny! It was very heavy, and he wondered if he could fly in such a heavy thing!

"Silly Sammy!!" teased his mother as she tickled him. "The raincoat is made for you. See the holes for your wings? You can fly just fine with the coat on. I'll leave it in your bedroom for now."

Sammy still did not like the coat.

Soon it was bedtime and daddy tucked Sammy into bed. As he shut the door he said, "It is a fine coat, Sammy!"

The slick, bright yellow raincoat caught the light from the streetlamp on the other side of the park. Sammy poked it a few times, but it did not move from his bed.

On Monday morning, Sammy slid out of his bed and opened the curtains to a sunny summer's day!

"Yay!" he yelled. He wouldn't have to wear the slick, bright yellow raincoat today!

Sammy smiled as he ate breakfast. His smile got even bigger as he brushed his teeth. He could leave the coat behind today!

As Sammy headed to the front door his mom stopped him and asked where his coat was. Sammy said, "In my closet because I won't need it today!"

"It will rain later today, honey. You do not have to wear the raincoat now, but I will put it in your backpack just in case it rains. I want you to be warm and dry so you can fly if it rains."

Sammy groaned.

Sammy put his backpack on, and it was VERY heavy! He wobbled as he flew to school. In fact, he wobbled so much he tumbled onto the feet of Mr. Squirrel, who was enjoying his breakfast on a tree branch.

"Why Sammy, you startled me! Are you all right?" asked Mr. Squirrel.

"Yes, thank you," Sammy said as he picked up the books that had spilled out in a jumble when he took a tumble. "I have a new raincoat and it is very heavy to carry in my backpack!"

"Oh, I see that now!" said Mr. Squirrel. "Don't worry Sammy, I know how well you fly! You will soon get the hang of it!"

Sammy had a lot of fun at school that day! The sun shone brightly, and he played with his friends. He flew home with the raincoat still folded in his backpack. He told his mother how wobbly he flew and how he had tumbled into Mr. Squirrel! She said he did just fine, and he should go play with his younger sister until dinner was ready.

Sammy woke the next morning to a loud crash of thunder! "Oh no!" Sammy thought.

It was raining, and Sammy did not like that!

Not one bit!

As he got ready for school mom told him to wear the raincoat.

He wobbled even more today because his backpack slid on the slick, bright yellow raincoat. Sammy did not like that!

Not at all!

Mr. Squirrel smiled and waved as Sammy wobbled by on his way to school. Sammy called out that he did not like his coat! Not at all!

Mr. Squirrel laughed out loud and said, "It is better than a soggy tail!" Sammy did not know what that meant, but he was already too far away to ask Mr. Squirrel.

It rained during recess! It rained during lunch!! It rained during classes!!!

The rain showed no signs of stopping! It was raining when the school bell rang at the end of the day!

Sammy put the slick, bright yellow raincoat on and loaded his backpack before heading back home.

As he flew, he saw Mrs. Robin and called out hello. She landed nearby and said hello as well.

"That's a very nice raincoat you have Sammy! I wish I had one to wear."

"I think you would find it very smelly and slippery Mrs. Robin!" Sammy replied. "It weighs so much, and you would wobble when you fly! You would even tumble when you land!"

Mrs. Robin sniffed the air and said she could not smell a thing! She shook her wings and water drops went everywhere!

"Your mother must love you a lot to have bought you a coat that keeps you so warm and dry!" she said as she flew off.

Sammy thought about that as he watched Mrs. Robin fly away.

"Dinner! Oh no! I will be late if I don't hurry up!"

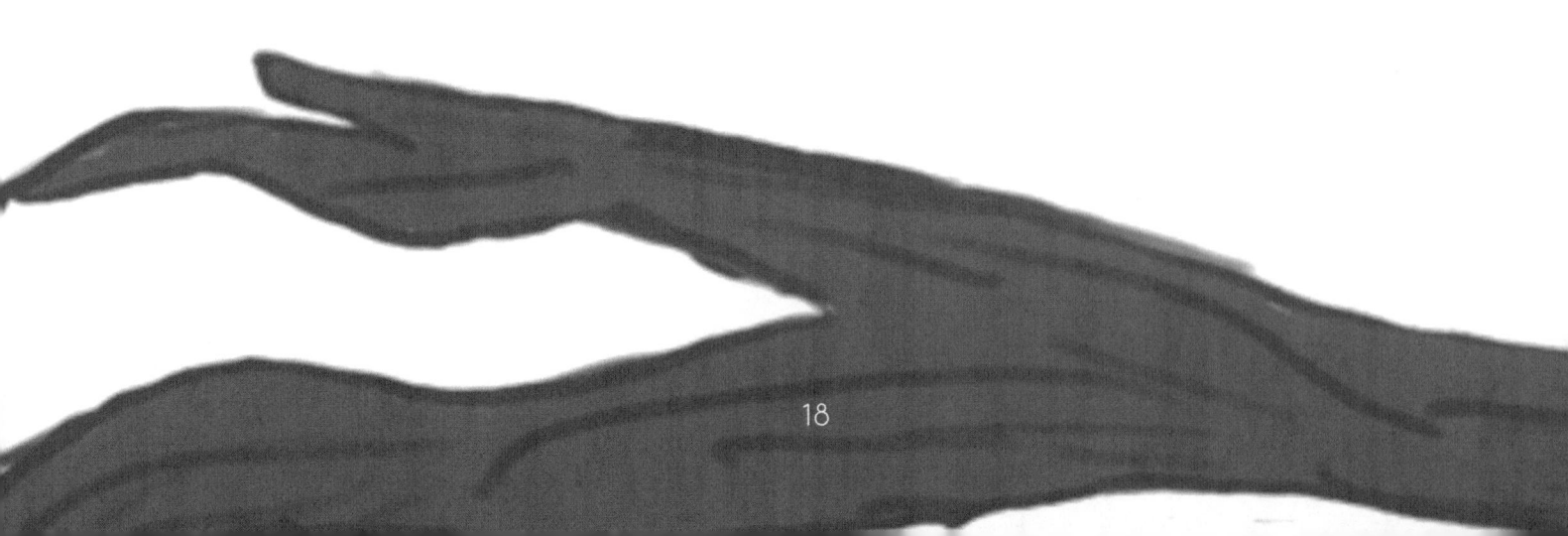

Mommy greeted Sammy as he came into the house. His coat was as wet as could be, so he took it off and hung it up. His mom smiled and said, "See, the raincoat is all wet, but you are warm and dry!"

Sammy looked at his feet and said,
"Yeah, I guess."

It rained again the next day!

It rained the day after that!!

It rained after that one too!!!

It rained all week!

Sammy thought it was never going to stop raining!

He worried that the big game would have to be called off!

That Saturday morning, as Sammy and his sister played in her room, their mother came in and told Sammy it was time to get ready for the big baseball game. For now, the rain finally stopped and the sun was shining! It was time to play baseball!

The sun was brightly shining as the game started. The visiting team scored a home run in the first inning, taking the lead!

"Oh no!" Sammy grumbled to himself. "They are better than I thought they were."

It began raining just as the Gnats tagged out the 3rd runner in the 9th inning.

The score was 7-6. Sammy didn't like that his team was losing!

The Gnats had a chance at winning, though!

The Gnats had two outs with a runner on third when Sammy heard that he was up to bat.

As Sammy gulped and reached for his favorite bat, he noticed that it had just started to rain. He was nervous because if he struck out, the game would be over, and his team would lose.

As he walked out into the pouring rain, he could hear his mother yell at him to put on his raincoat!

He thought about how hard it would be to swing the bat while wearing the heavy raincoat and did not understand why all his teammates had put on their raincoats. He decided not to put on his raincoat; he wanted his team to win. He looked at his mother and shook his head.

"Batter up!" yelled Mr. Squirrel as he motioned Sammy to get ready.

Three strikes and Sammy was out! He was the last batter. His team lost the game!

As he slowly walked back to the dugout with his head hung low, Sammy was glad he would at least be out of the cold rain.

The game ended with a final score of 7-6.

Sammy did not like that!

Not at all!

The sunshine came back as everyone was packing up to head home.

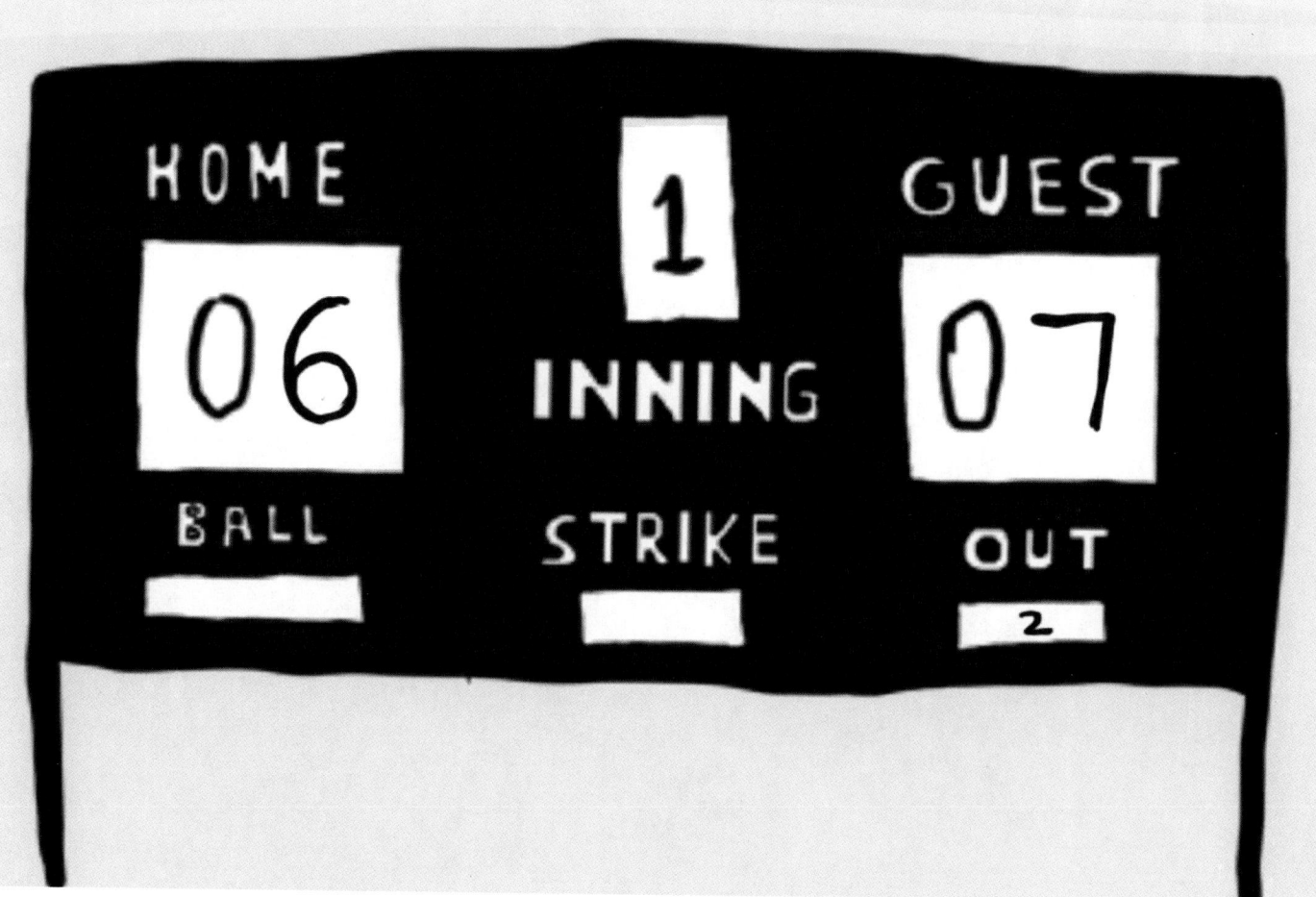

Sammy's teeth chattered as he walked over to his family in the stands. His dad ruffled Sammy's wet hair and said, "You did great today. Next time you'll win!"

Sammy knew he would have done better if he had just put on his raincoat.

"Mother and I need to start dinner for you and your sister, so we are going to fly home," Dad said.

Sammy realized he was still too wet and cold to fly home with them, so he decided he would walk home with his friends.

Sammy watched his parents fly off, and then headed over to where his friends were.

Sammy asked if anyone wanted to walk home with him, but no one could. They all had to fly home with their parents.

Sammy realized he was the only one that was too wet and cold to fly.

He had to walk home alone.

Sammy sighed as his mom tucked him into bed later that night.

"What's wrong?" Mother asked him.

"I should have listened to you and wore my raincoat. Because I didn't, I lost the baseball game and couldn't fly home with you and Daddy," Sammy replied. "I'm so sorry!"

"Sweetie, Daddy and I only want what is best for you," said mom. "We know you don't like the raincoat, but we want you to stay warm and dry when it rains. When you are warm and dry, you can enjoy rainy days just as much as you do those beautiful sunny days when you are playing with your friends."

Mommy kissed him and got up to leave his bedroom. Sammy sighed and rolled over. "It will never stop raining!" he said to himself as a tear hit his pillow.

Sammy got up Monday morning and he just knew it would be raining.

He sighed as he got dressed. He sighed as he ate breakfast.

Sammy just knew it would rain again today!

Mom laced up Sammy's shoes and he sighed once again as he reached for the slick, bright yellow raincoat.

"Silly Sammy!" Mom said. "You won't need your coat today. See how sunny it is?" At that, she opened the front door to show him the bright sunshine.

Sammy yipped and smiled as he grabbed his backpack. He took a few steps, then turned back around. "Can you please pack my raincoat, just in case?"

"Absolutely!" Mom said with a smile.

He waved at Mr. Squirrel.

He waved at Mrs. Robin.

He did not even notice he flew without a wobble.

Manufactured by Amazon.ca
Bolton, ON